STORYTIME COLLECTION

This book belongs to

_____

_____

Autumn
Publishing

Published in 2020
by Autumn Publishing
Cottage Farm
Sywell
NN6 0BJ
www.igloobooks.com

Autumn is an imprint of Bonnier Books UK

© 2019 MARVEL

0920 004
4 6 8 10 9 7 5 3
ISBN 978-1-78905-846-8

Printed and manufactured in China

FROM HERE TO INFINITY

Once again, Loki had been defeated by the Avengers in his latest attempt to lure his brother Thor into battle and to steal the throne of Asgard from him.

"You'll stay in prison until your trial," Thor said, as he slammed the prison gate shut.

"As you command, dear brother," Loki replied with a sneer.

He might be physically trapped in the Asgard prison cell, but that wouldn't stop Loki playing his mind games with people to get what he wanted.

And he knew exactly who he could trick to get revenge on his brother.

As soon as Thor left, Loki closed his eyes and used his magic powers to locate Dr Bruce Banner in his home village on Earth.

Dr Banner suddenly found himself under attack from a crowd of vicious warriors. This was just Loki's trick, but the scientist didn't know that the warriors were really peaceful villagers.

Dr Banner became angry and transformed into the Hulk. He started chasing the terrified villagers and destroying buildings.

Back at Avengers Tower, Nick Fury, head of S.H.I.E.L.D., had been informed of Hulk's attack. And just as Loki had planned, he called on his mighty team.

"AVENGERS ASSEMBLE!"

Iron Man, Captain America, Black Widow and Hawkeye quickly flew to the village in a S.H.I.E.L.D. Quinjet.

"Don't worry," Iron Man said to the frightened villagers, "we're here to help. Which way did he go?"

Meanwhile, Thor hurried
from Asgard to help the rest
of the team.

In his prison cell, Loki grinned
to himself. "So predictable, brother.
You can never resist trying to save
the day!"

As soon as Thor arrived at the
village, Loki used his magic to create
an image of Hulk. Thor swung his
hammer as Hulk charged at him,
but his hammer went straight
through the illusion.

"Up to your old tricks again,
Loki," Thor said. "You won't get
away with this!" He raced back to
Asgard, grabbed his adopted brother,
and flew back to Earth with him.

On Earth, the other Avengers had found the real Hulk. Loki used his magic once again to make Hulk think that they were about to attack him.

"Easy there, big fella!" said Captain America, as Hulk grabbed his shield and lashed out at Iron Man.

"Stop fighting!" shouted Thor, landing in the middle of the battle.
"Loki is the one to blame for this mess."

Hulk moved towards Loki, but Loki had one more trick up his sleeve.
He created many illusions of himself, so that Hulk couldn't tell which
Loki was real.

Hulk swung his huge arm in a wide circle, his fist going through each fake Loki until he hit the real one. Loki fell to the ground.

"Your fun is over," said Thor. "It's back to prison for you, brother."

Back at S.H.I.E.L.D. headquarters, the Avengers were celebrating their victory when Nick Fury called them into a meeting.

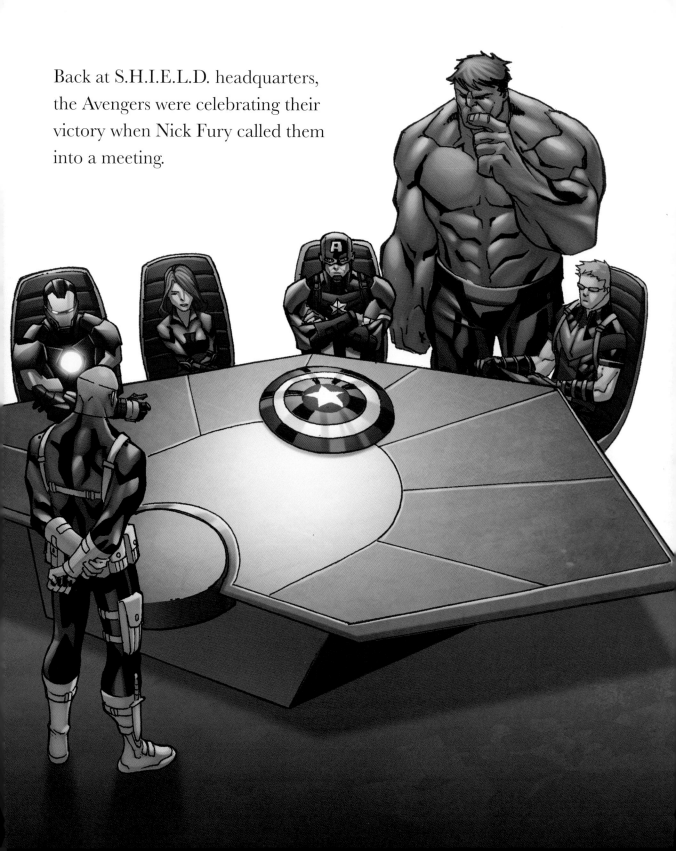

"Avengers," said Nick Fury, "one of the Infinity Stones has gone missing…"

The Infinity Stones were six gems. Whoever had all of them gained magical superpowers. S.H.I.E.L.D. had been trying to stop them falling into the wrong hands for years.

"… and I know who took it – **THANOS**. He's been spotted in Central Park."

The Avengers rushed to Central Park. Thanos held five of the Infinity Stone gems in one of his giant hands. He fitted them into slots in the gauntlet he was wearing on the other hand.

"Behold," he roared, "the Infinity Gauntlet!"

The giant Super Villain blasted them with energy beams from the gauntlet, but Captain America deflected the blast back at Thanos as the rest of the team surrounded him, ready to attack.

Thanos knew he couldn't fight all five Avengers, so he teleported away.

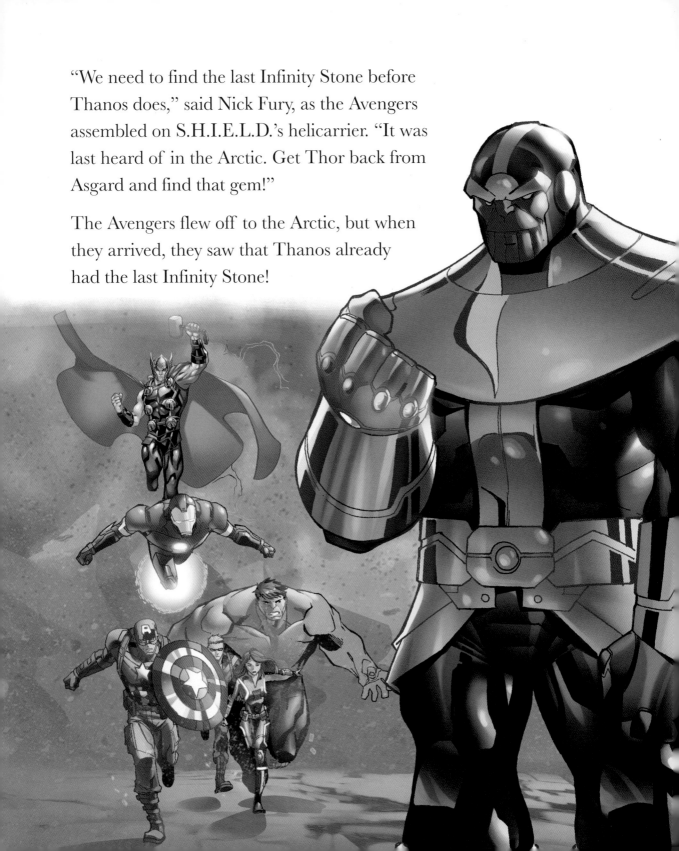

"We need to find the last Infinity Stone before Thanos does," said Nick Fury, as the Avengers assembled on S.H.I.E.L.D.'s helicarrier. "It was last heard of in the Arctic. Get Thor back from Asgard and find that gem!"

The Avengers flew off to the Arctic, but when they arrived, they saw that Thanos already had the last Infinity Stone!

The Avengers watched
as Thanos placed the stone
into the Infinity Gauntlet,
alongside the other five gems.

"You're too late, Avengers,"
Thanos laughed. "Nothing can
stop me now!"

"We'll see about that,"
said Captain America.

"He's too strong for us individually," shouted Iron Man. "Somehow, we need to break the Infinity Gauntlet."

"What if we combine our powers?" Captain America suggested.

"Great idea!" said Thor. He raised his magic hammer and called on the power of lightning to take over Captain America's shield. Then, Iron Man used Hawkeye's arrows and Black Widow's bracelets to transfer the power of his chest arc reactor to the shield.

"Okay, big guy," said Iron Man, "it's over to you!"

Hulk took Captain America's energy-filled shield and hurled it towards the Infinity Gauntlet on Thanos's raised fist.

BLAST! There was a huge explosion and the gauntlet fell to the ground. Black Widow grabbed all the fallen gems.

"Hulk **SMASH!**" roared Hulk, as he destroyed what was left of the Infinity Gauntlet.

Thanos was defeated! But before the Avengers could grab him, he disappeared.

Back at headquarters, Black Widow handed the six Infinity Stones to Nick Fury for safekeeping.

"It's a shame we didn't catch Thanos," she said. "But he'll be back, and next time we'll be ready for him!"

"And ready for any threat against Earth!" added Iron Man.

THE LEGEND OF THE
BLACK PANTHER

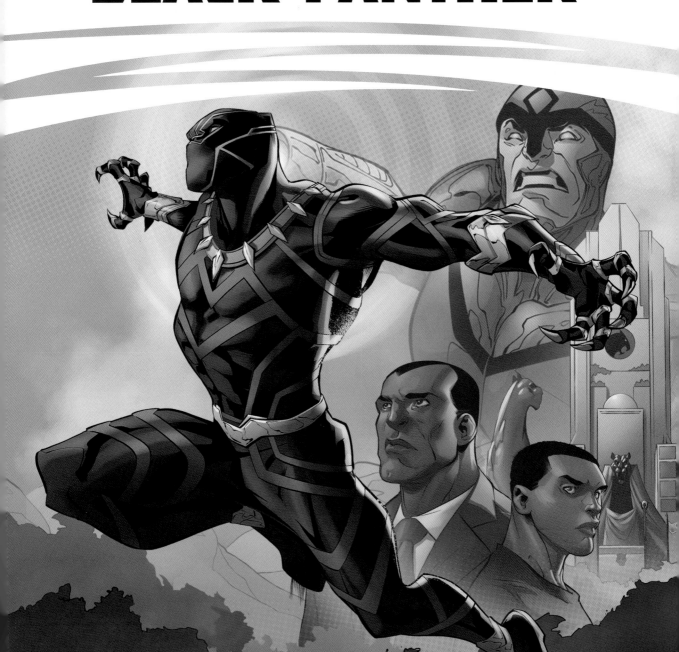

King T'Challa sighed with relief as his Royal Jet
flew low over the lush jungle treetops of Wakanda,
his African home. He had been away for a long
time, working with the Avengers as Super Hero
Black Panther, stopping crime and fighting for
justice. T'Challa enjoyed working with a team, but
now he needed some time alone to think.

T'Challa had never felt comfortable as king.
The role and all its responsibilities did not come
easily to him, but he had promised to honour his
father's legacy. His father had been a great leader
and protector, and T'Challa missed him every day.

"Welcome home, my son," said Ramonda, as T'Challa entered the palace. She hugged him tightly. "I know this is difficult for you and that you miss your father, but you don't need to be the king your father was. You are to be the king that you are meant to be."

T'Challa smiled at his mother and was just about to recount his adventures with the Avengers, when the doors burst open. It was Okoye, leader of the warrior women, the Dora Milaje, whose job it was to protect the Wakandan king.

"Sire, an emergency!" she shouted.

"We're being hit by earthquakes across the country from
unknown sources," Okoye said, as T'Challa, Ramonda and
the Tribe elders gathered in the council room. "They are
causing floods and the volcano has started to erupt."

"What are we to do, sire?" Okoye asked.

The tribal elders turned to look at T'Challa. He saw his mother's kind face and remembered her words: you are to be the king you are meant to be.

"Okoye, get the Dora Milaje to start evacuating everyone in the danger zones," said T'Challa. "Mother, speak to the Wakandan people to reassure and calm them."

T'Challa ran to the door, looking grim. "I am going to stop the person behind this!" he growled.

T'Challa knew exactly who was causing the earthquakes. There was only one person who had ever successfully infiltrated Wakanda – the evil Super Villain responsible for his father's death.

"Klaw is back!" T'Challa cried as he left the palace.

Meanwhile, Ramonda went to address the people of Wakanda from the palace balcony. "There is no need to panic. The Black Panther is on his way to stop the villain behind all this destruction."

The people of Wakanda cheered. With Black Panther on the case, they knew they had nothing to fear.

Wakanda was famous for its special metal, Vibranium, which could absorb sound waves and other vibrations. In fact, Black Panther's suit was made from Vibranium.

Black Panther went straight to the Vibranium mines. He was determined to bring his father's killer to justice.

"Load up all these trucks with the Vibranium rods," he shouted to the workers. "We will cut Klaw off on his way to the city!"

When the fleet of trucks reached the outskirts of the city, Black Panther ordered them to form a long line. He scanned the land ahead of them.

"Look! There!" he shouted. The ground in the distance was being ripped apart by pink, sonic energy. Black Panther raised his arm and called out to the workers in the trucks, "He's almost here. Get ready…"

"NOW!" screamed Black Panther, when the sonic energy was a couple of metres away.

BOOM! THUMP! KA-TANG!

The trucks roared to life and slammed their solid Vibranium rods straight down into the ground.

SMASH! Klaw crashed into the rods underground. As they absorbed all his sonic energy, Klaw was blasted out of the earth.

"Ha! You don't think you can beat me that easily do you, Black Panther?" laughed Klaw, as he squared off with his enemy.

Black Panther knew that destroying Klaw's sonic converter, even if it was nearly unbreakable, was the key to defeating him.

A good leader always has a backup plan, Black Panther thought to himself.

"I'm not done with you yet, Klaw!"

Black Panther lunged at Klaw, but the superhuman villain was quick and spun away from the attack.

"Ah, you fight honourably, one-on-one, as your father did. But your father was just a man, and so are you. I destroyed your father, and I will destroy you!" laughed Klaw. Suddenly a giant sonic octopus appeared. "Get ready to be crushed!"

Black Panther managed to dodge all the creature's arms, but then Klaw pinned him to the ground.

"You have lost the battle, T'Challa, just like your father," taunted Klaw.

"No, actually, you have. I just needed to get you into position," said Black Panther.

Before Klaw could wonder what Black Panther meant, the Super Hero thrust his powerful legs forwards. The force of the blow sent Klaw flying through the air…

… and right into two half-spheres made
of Vibranium that snapped in place around
Klaw, trapping him.

"My father would never have asked for
help from his people," said Black Panther.
"He insisted on doing everything for himself.
I admired him for that. But I am not my
father. The Wakandan people are not only my
responsibility, they are also my greatest allies."

He waved to the workers in the trucks.

"Thank you for all your help. Now take this
monster away."

"This isn't over, Black Panther!" shouted Klaw
from his Vibranium prison. "I'll be back!"

Tired but happy, T'Challa returned
to the palace and crossed the
platform in front of the entrance.

The people of Wakanda crowded around him and chanted, **"BLACK PANTHER! BLACK PANTHER!"**

"Sire, as soon as you trapped Klaw, the earthquakes stopped," said Okoye. "All has returned to normal."

T'Challa breathed a sigh of relief. He walked over to Ramonda and kneeled down before her. "Mother, thank you for believing in me, as always," he said.

"It wasn't the Black Panther who saved Wakanda today," Ramonda said softly to her son. "It was the quick thinking of T'Challa, King of Wakanda. Today you have found your own path."

The Wakandans chanted again, but this time, **"T'Challa! T'Challa!"**

T'Challa smiled. For the first time in his life, he knew he was worthy to wear both the crown of Wakanda and the mantle of the Black Panther.

The Avengers were gathered on the roof of Avengers Tower.

"Something unspeakable has happened," Iron Man informed them. "The Internet is down!"

"Oh, no!" gasped Falcon. "All vital Earth systems need the Internet. Hospitals, the electric grid, you name it."

Captain America stepped forwards. "While the rest of you see what you can do to help, Iron Man and I will find out who is behind this cyber crime."

"Way ahead of you, Cap," said Iron Man. **"JARVIS** has come up with one name – Ultron! It looks like that Artificial Intelligence has released a virus into the network."

"I think we might need a little extra help on this one," decided Captain America. "We need Captain Marvel."

"I've heard of her," said Iron Man. "But who exactly is she?"

"She's head of Alpha Flight," replied Captain America. "She's an astronaut, half-alien, and won't back down for anyone. Oh, and she lives in the Statue of Liberty's crown."

When they arrived at the Statue of Liberty, Captain Marvel was waiting for them.

"The Internet is down across the globe. It's complete chaos," she said, jumping straight to the point.

"Ultron released a virus," explained Iron Man.

"I'm on it," said Captain Marvel. "Meet me at Alpha Flight Headquarters." Then, not waiting to see if they were following, she launched herself into the sky.

The three heroes soared through the air and soon arrived at Alpha Flight Headquarters. The place was buzzing with electronic activity.

"Their communication systems don't appear to be down," noted Captain America.

"They must have bypassed the traditional network systems," replied Iron Man.

The two Avengers watched in admiration as Captain Marvel began issuing orders.

"Gonzalez!" she said. "Get an encrypted pipeline. O'Connell! Initiate offensive network protocol 616."

Soon, lines of code were scrolling across the screens.

"It's digital warfare," explained Iron Man. "She's hunting Ultron's virus." He turned to Captain Marvel. "Ultron will know where this is coming from," Iron Man warned her. "He'll come and shut us down."

"Let him come," smiled Captain Marvel. And just at that moment – **BOOM!** – Ultron exploded through the wall behind Captain America.

"How cute," he snarled, grabbing Cap's shield. "Iron Man and Captain America think they can foil my plot to destroy human civilization."

Captain America hit Ultron with a mighty punch, but Ultron was too powerful. He tossed Captain America through the hole in the wall. Then, he turned on Iron Man. "Give up, puny humans. Nobody can protect humanity now."

Iron Man began to laugh. "You've never met my friend Captain Marvel, have you?"

Ultron quickly turned on Captain Marvel and sneered. "I'll soon destroy this puny human woman."

"I'm only half human," said Captain Marvel, swinging a well-aimed punch at the cyber pest's face.

Ultron tackled her to the ground and the pair crashed around Alpha Flight Headquarters in deadly combat.

In the background, the computers whirred with activity. Then, **BING!** They announced that their job was done. The virus was destroyed.

"There you go," smiled Captain Marvel. "Your virus is toast, Ultron, and so are you."

She swung an almighty punch that catapulted Ultron out through the wall and hurled him into space!

"What'd I miss?" asked Captain America,
as he staggered back into the Headquarters.

"Oh, nothing much," laughed Iron Man, removing his mask and giving Captain Marvel a high five. "The Internet's back up and Ultron's out of our hair. Sorry, Cap, but it looks like the Avengers have a new Captain!"

COLLECT THEM ALL!

With 13 more exciting titles to choose from, you'll want to complete your Storytime Collection!

Can Aladdin and Jasmine stop the evil Jafar?

Will Bambi learn the value of friendship?

Will Belle be able to break the curse?

Will Dory finally find her parents?

How far will a father go for his son?

Can Anna and Elsa stop an eternal winter?

Will Mowgli defeat Shere Khan?

Will the Incredibles save the day?

Will Simba ever become king?

Will Ariel be able to find her prince in time?

Can Moana restore the heart of Te Fiti?

Will Maleficent's curse come true?

Will Rapunzel learn who she truly is?